Finding True Love

THE DR. CAGE CHRONICLES:
MEMOIRS OF A SEX THERAPIST

Finding True Love

GRAYSON ACE

4 Horsemen
Publications, Inc.

Chapter 1

After the video of me and Austin went viral and all of the appointment requests came in, I knew I had no choice but to hire more therapists. Rocky wasn't quite ready to take on such an important role, so I posted the job on a few websites, and I swear I didn't even hit submit when the applications started flying in.

It was hard to focus on my work and hiring therapists when I couldn't get over what Austin had done to me. I literally couldn't believe it. He and I had such a whirlwind romance, or at least I thought it was a romance. I needed to accept that I was never going to get the closure that I deserved from him, nor would I ever hear from him again. It was hard to admit, but for the first time, I felt like I was heartbroken.

I spent several weeks just kind of moping around. I cancelled and entire weeks' worth of patients and had Rocky cover for some of them. He came home nearly every day telling me that I wouldn't believe what my patients let him do to them, but I didn't even want to hear it. He really shouldn't have even been seeing the patients, especially the way I saw them, but I really didn't care at that point.

My friends are what really kept me going through all of this, especially Jackie. One Friday night, she texted me, and that text changed everything.

[Jackie: Get the fuck out of bed and get dressed. We're going shopping.]

Within 20 minutes, she was honking the horn, and I ran out the front door and jumped in. I could tell by what she was wearing that we weren't going to the mall. And within minutes we were walking into Swinging Richards.

Jackie always knew how to cheer me up. Sitting at the bar with my favorite cocktail, watching the guys on stage twirl their dongs, and just laughing our asses off, for the first time in weeks, I was beginning to feel like myself again. Jackie walked away to take a phone call, and these two hunks walked up and started talking to me. They recognized who I was and told me that they had both just graduated with their degrees and had applied to my clinic. I normally would have asked to see their resume, but by the looks of them, I knew they'd both understand how I operate. The one guy looked familiar, but I couldn't tell if he had been a patient of mine, or maybe someone that Rocky had brought home. I gave them my card and told them to both meet me at the office at noon the following day for interviews.

Jackie came back in and asked why I had such a big smile on my face. I told her the best way to get over someone was to get under someone else. We nearly dropped our drinks we were laughing so hard, but little did she know—I was serious.

Chapter 2

hen I got to the office the next day, the two guys were already waiting outside. I invited them inside and took them back to one of the therapy rooms, having them both sit down. I normally would have interviewed them individually, but knew how it was going to end up, so it was just easier to start with both of them present.

I had each of them tell me about their background, experiences, and most importantly, why they wanted to work for me. They looked at each other and smiled.

"Instead of telling you, we want to show you."

I realized that I hadn't even learned their names yet, and I was going to want those so I knew whose name I could scream out.

Chris and Danny. Easy enough.

Chris got up off the couch and knelt down in front of Danny. He pulled his pants down while Danny took off his shirt. Chris grabbed his cock and started sucking on it, and Danny rubbed his hands down his back and toward the top of his ass. I could see that Danny had a pretty thick cock, and I'm assuming that was why Chris started with him instead of me— they'd obviously done this before.

Chris sucked on Danny's cock for about five or six minutes, and then turned around and looked at me. At this point, I was already rubbing my own boner—it was impossible not to get hard watching this. Chris looked at me and said, "What are you waiting for? Come join us." I started unzipping my pants and Chris turned around and crawled over toward me, forcing himself in between my legs. He grabbed onto my cock and immediately swallowed the entire thing.

I looked over at Danny who had started stroking his dick. Chris was bobbing his head up and down as fast as he could. His mouth was so warm and went, and he would tease the tip before sucking on just the head, and then devouring my entire rod.

He kept bobbing his head up and down, taking every inch I had to offer. He would start going faster before slowing down again. For a minute, I completely forgot that Danny was even there until he got up and walked over next to my chair, forcing his massive tool right into my face. Without hesitation, I grabbed onto his piece, and he grabbed the back of my head, shoving himself completely into my throat, making me really gag. I had one hand on Chris's head as he bounced up and down, and another stroking Danny's dick as it went in and out of my mouth.

We kept sucking on each other's cocks for several minutes before Danny got down on the ground next to Chris to share mine. They each took a side of the shaft and were rubbing their lips and tongues up and down. One would put my entire piece in their mouth while the other would suck on my balls and go down toward my hole, and then they'd switch positions. After a few minutes, I told them it was time for one of them to bottom.

Chris said that he wanted me to fuck him first and get him nice and loosened up. I took off my shirt while Chris pulled off the rest of my pants, and we moved over to the couch. I sat down and lubed up my cock, and then poured some lube on my finger to get Chris's hole nice and wet. Danny sat down next to me and started stroking my cock while I was getting Chris ready.

Chris straddled me and slowly started sitting down until the head of my penis was touching his hole. He lowered his ass a little more, and I could feel just how tight his hole was as my head entered it. He let out a scream, and I couldn't believe how amazing his hole felt.

Danny was sitting back and stroking his cock in pure excitement. Chris lowered himself a little more, and with each inch of my dick that disappeared inside of him, he would let out another moan. It took a few minutes, but my cock had finally disappeared in his ass, and he just sat there for a minute and started making out with me before starting to move his ass up and down.

He started out pretty slow, and then started going faster and faster. Danny leaned over and started sucking on Chris's cock while he was riding me, and the moans and sounds coming out of his mouth were unlike any other. This was like popping a guy's cherry, and it was fucking amazing.

After a few minutes, Chris said that it was Danny's turn. Chris got off my cock, stood up, and pushed Danny so that he was leaning over me. Danny started making out with me, getting on all fours and inviting Chris to stick his dick in his ass. Chris bent down and stuck his tongue in Danny's ass, getting it nice and wet while he was lubing up his own cock. Danny was a pretty good kisser and put his head down and started sucking on my cock.

Danny didn't even seem to flinch as Chris shoved his monster inside of him. Once Chris had his piece completely engulfed by Danny's hole, he grabbed his hips and immediately started rough fucking him. Danny was still sucking on my dick, so his moans had a mouthful in them.

I pulled Danny's head up from sucking on my dick and slid down off the couch in front of him and started sucking on his cock. Who in the world wouldn't cum from getting fucked and sucked at the same time? He was still on all fours and using the couch to hold him up, so I had pretty easy access to his massive dick.

I let that entire thing go back into my mouth and stroked and sucked it until I could feel it start throbbing.

Danny let out a loud moan and said, "I'm going to blow!" Chris kept pounding away and I kept sucking on it. He blew such a huge load in my mouth that I couldn't even swallow all of it—most of it came exploding out of my mouth. I kept sucking, though, because I wanted to get every last drop. To my surprise, he let Chris continue fucking him for a few minutes while I wiped my face off. I noticed that Danny's cock was still rock hard and knew it was time for a swap.

I leaned over the side of the couch and told Chris to come up behind me and start fucking me, and then Danny got behind him. Chris put his dick in me but waited to start thrusting until Danny was inside of him. I could feel the moment that Danny shoved his cock in Chris's hole because Chris's dick inside of me felt like it grew the same moment.

Chris, being in the middle, did most of the motions, and was letting out some pretty loud sounds. I couldn't help but moan myself because his cock in my hole felt pretty amazing. I moved forward so that Chris's dick would slide out of my hole so that the two of them could fuck for a little bit while I sucked on Chris's cock.

Danny pushed Chris's head down into the couch, grabbed his hips, and started thrusting his cock in and out of his hole. I got in front of Chris and started sucking on him. After a few minutes, Chris pulled me back up and said he was getting close to cumming and wanted to cum in my hole.

I got back on the edge of the couch, this time on my back, and let Chris lift my legs above his shoulders and slide his wet member back inside of me. Danny immediately started pounding away, and not even twenty seconds later, Chris busted out, "I'm gonna nut." Danny started pounding harder, and as soon as that milk started shooting out of Chris's dick, I could feel my hole getting flooded. Chris gave a few more good pumps inside of me, and then I heard Danny say, "I'm gonna blow again." I was shocked because I didn't think he was going to cum again, but then again, also not super surprised.

Danny gave Chris's hole a few more good thrusts and then let out a massive scream. At the same time, I saw Chris's body shake as his hole was being filled with Danny's load. Danny kept pumping it inside of him until he knew his cock was completely drained, and then pulled his dick out. He came around Chris and knelt down in front of me and said, "Your turn."

His cock was still covered in cum, and he shoved it right inside my hole and started pounding away. I'm not sure how this guy still had anything left in him, but he was ready to give it to me. Chris came over and started stroking my cock, and I couldn't even give warning when I shot my load straight up and over my head. Danny pulled his dick out and Chris bent down to suck the rest of the cum off of it, and then started licking all the cum off my chest.

There was no doubt in my mind that these two guys would be able to handle the majority of my patients. I asked if they could start the following week, but they were eager to start immediately. I put my clothes back on and tossed them the keys.

"Make sure you lock up when you're done."

And I knew they'd probably be going for round 2 once I had left.

Chapter 3

With the addition of Chris and Danny to the practice, it was going to be a lot easier for me to take a step back and really figure things out. I wanted to get back into the dating scene and was ready to meet someone, especially after my fiasco with Austin. There was this guy that I had met online and was talking to for a few weeks. His name was Jordan, and he was a bit of a preppy looking guy. He was tall, blonde hair, and super cute. He liked sending goofy Snapchat stories and really just made me laugh. He was a huge theme park fanatic, so we decided to meet at a theme park about two hours away for our first date.

I decided to make a weekend out of it and invited Jackie along with me. We booked a hotel with an amazing pool, and she just hung out while I went and met Jordan at the theme park. He was just as funny in person as he was on the phone. We rode a few rides, had some cocktails, and just spent most of the day talking. There was a little flirtation happening, but nothing too heavy.

We decided to make our way out of the theme park and talked about meeting later that night for dinner and drinks. I thought they date went pretty well and was excited to see him again. I told him I wanted to go back to the hotel and relax and freshen up and that I'd call him when I was heading to the restaurant.

When I was on my way to meet him, I tried calling, but he didn't answer. I sent him a text but figured he was probably in the shower, so I continued on to the restaurant. I sat in my car when I got there and called him again, but still no answer. After a few more messages and waiting in the parking lot for 45 minutes, I gave up and headed back to the hotel.

I really didn't have time for games like this. I sent him a pretty nasty message, basically saying if he wasn't interested, all he needed to do was say so. Rejection didn't bother me. Being inconsiderate did. I told Jackie what happened and just forgot about him. The next morning I had a message from him apologizing, claiming that he fell asleep when he got home and didn't wake up until around 11pm. I told him he should have texted me when he woke up rather than waiting for the morning. I then lectured him for about ten minutes on why it wasn't okay, told him to go fuck himself, and blocked him.

Jackie and I spent the rest of the weekend just hanging around the pool and relaxing. It was exactly what I needed to recharge and refresh my mind. I, of course, was scrolling through the apps and matched with another guy who lived about a half hour away from me. There was something different about him. His name was Wayne, and he was purely handsome.

He had a nice smile and these gorgeous blue eyes, and we spent nearly the entire weekend chatting and made plans to meet for dinner on Monday night when I got back.

I was really excited about meeting Wayne. There was something special about him, and even without meeting him, I felt completely at ease. I went shopping Monday afternoon for a new outfit, and Wayne asked if I wanted to meet at a little Italian restaurant on the beach, which just happened to be one of my favorite places. It's like we were just vibing without even really knowing one another.

As I was getting ready for our date, I started feeling a little light-headed, and immediately knew something was wrong. I grabbed the thermometer and took my temperature, which was coming in at 101. I started crying. How was this happening to me? I immediately video chatted Wayne. I knew I didn't look sick and didn't want him to think I was backing out on our date, but I knew with my fever that I couldn't risk seeing him. Luckily, he was super understanding, and I told him I'd call him the next day to chat.

I went to the doctor the following morning, and he confirmed what I was afraid of.

I was positive for Covid.

I started crying again. I was scared and didn't know what was going to happen. I also had no clue how I had gotten sick. I was starting to get a sore throat and was feeling really tired. I sent a picture of my test results to Wayne so that he knew I really didn't intend on missing our first date. We kept texting throughout the day, whenever I was awake, which really wasn't all that much.

By the next day, I thought I was going to die. I was having trouble breathing and couldn't even get out of bed. I texted Wayne when I woke up and told him I was going to the hospital. He was super worried and asked if there was anything he could do. I would have loved to have his company but knew that I couldn't. I drove myself to the ER, and they admitted me and put me on oxygen for the next two days. I told Wayne I was going to keep my phone off because I just didn't have much energy, and it seemed like the longest two days of my life.

When I got home a few days later, there were flowers waiting for me at my house. I'm not sure how he did it, but Wayne managed to find my address. It was so sweet of him, yet a little startling that he could find my address so quickly. I called him and thanked him. I was feeling a million times better but was still testing positive, so I asked if we could "virtual date" while I was recovering.

We started having nightly video chats. We would order dinner from the same restaurant, or watch the same movie, as if we were physically together. It was really nice to get to know him this way without the pressure of physically being together. Our talks would occasionally get a little dirty, and one night he sent me a nice dick pic with the caption, "I wish it was inside of you." I could tell he was a top and couldn't wait to have his thick monster fill my hole. I, of course, responded with my own dick pic, and within ten seconds, he sent a video shooting his load all over his chest, and I knew I needed to get better as fast as I could.

We virtually dated for another week before I finally started testing negative. As soon as I got those negative test results, we made plans to finally meet at that Italian restaurant. I was nervous and excited all at the same time. When I pulled into the parking lot and saw him waiting at the door, I had butterflies in my stomach. He was even more handsome in person that he was in his pictures. I walked up to him and gave him a huge hug, him kissing me on the cheek, and we walked inside.

We must have sat and talked for nearly four hours, the conversation never ending. I could tell the staff were waiting for us to leave so they could shut down. Wayne walked me to my car and asked if I wanted to go back to his place for a drink, which of course I wanted to. He lived in a little condo right next to the beach, which was super charming.

He showed me around and poured me a glass of wine. He turned on the TV for some background noise and just happened to turn on one of my favorite shows. We talked a bit longer and then both became interested in the show. He grabbed onto my hand to hold it, and a few minutes later turned my face toward him and started kissing me. I quickly wrapped my arms around him and we started making out, and within a minute, I was straddling his lap, grabbing onto the back of his head to kiss him as passionately as I could.

I got up and held him by the hand, having him follow me to the bedroom. I could tell he was trying to hide his boner and just laughed a bit. He pushed me down on the bed and got on top of me, rubbing his boner against mine and shoving his tongue down my throat, moving over to my neck and sucking on it. I held onto his hips, pulling him closer to me. I really wanted him inside of me, but I also wanted to take our time.

We made out for about 20 more minutes, and then I rolled to the side and told him I needed to get home. I actually had an early day at the office and had a lot of catching up to do. I could tell he wasn't upset at all, and he asked when he could see me again. I told him I needed to go down to LA that weekend for a work event and asked if he wanted to go with me. It was crazy, but I felt like I had known him for a long time. He quickly said yes, and I told him I'd book him a flight and send the details.

As soon as I got home, I booked his flight and upgraded my hotel room since I knew we'd be spending most of the weekend in bed. Actually, I jerked off, and then booked his flight.

Chapter 4

Wayne met me at the airport that Friday night, and we made the quick flight down to LA. We checked into the hotel, and barely walked inside the room before he was pushing me up against the wall, shoving his tongue down my throat and rubbing his hands all over my chest.

He ripped my shirt off and started sucking on my nipples while I grabbed onto his hair. I thought we'd at least get dinner first, but I wasn't mad about it. I pushed him away and walked toward the bed and pulled him over to me. He leaned down and started kissing me, and I quickly grabbed his shirt and ripped it off. He wasn't ripped or anything but had a decent body with a little bit of a belly, which I find super sexy. He quickly got right on top of me, making out with his chest on top of mine, slightly grinding his dick on my leg. My hands were all over him, rubbing up and down his back and moving down toward his ass and into his shorts. He had a beautiful ass and it felt so good in my hands.

He would move from kissing my mouth to sucking on my neck, down to my nipples and back up again. I could feel his cock getting hard as he was rubbing it against my growing member. I reached down in between our bodies as we were grinding and started rubbing my hand on his dick. I knew he had a big cock, and now I was finally feeling it with my hands.

He started kissing down my neck and onto my chest and made his way down toward my happy trail with his mouth. He pulled my shorts and briefs down and devoured my whole piece with his mouth, not even grabbing onto it with his hands. I could feel my cock pressing against the back of his throat, and he didn't even let out a single gag—he was obviously a professional. He kept sucking up and down my shaft, and at one point pulled his own shorts down, releasing that beautiful monster.

He rolled over a bit on his side, never letting my dick escape from his mouth so he could start jerking on his own. I watched in a bit of awe as the rubbed his tool and knew I needed to get a taste of it. I grabbed his head and picked it up off of my cock and pulled him up toward me. We made out for a few seconds, and then I pulled him up even more to get his dick positioned right in front of my face. I pulled him closer, forcing his warm cock deep into my throat. I grabbed onto his ass cheeks and held them as he fucked my face, slowly at first and then faster as time went on. I reached down and started stroking my dick, letting his ram against the back of my throat without even caring.

After a few minutes, I pushed him off of me and onto his back and told him I wanted to feel him inside of me. I lubed up his cock, threw one leg over him and slowly lowered my ass down onto his pipe. I wasn't sure if I'd be able to take the entire thing, but it went into my hole with such ease—I didn't even need to give it a minute to stretch. I started bouncing up and down on his perfect cock. He leaned up from the pillow and started kissing me, and it was more like making love than fucking at that point.

I could feel his cock going deep into my ass and knew I wanted to take his load. I could tell from the look on his face that he wasn't used to the feeling of such a tight ass and wasn't going to last long. He grabbed onto my cock and started stroking it and said he was getting close. I leaned down to start kissing him again, and the moment our tongues touched, I felt him thrust upward and let out a screech, and I could feel his load filling my hole.

Wayne quickly pushed me off his dick and onto my back, lifted my legs and shoved his tongue into my hole. I was a bit surprised because he didn't seem like the type to want to eat his own cum out of a hole. He told me to push it out, and I could feel it dripping out of my hole, and him licking it all back up. I swear he must have emptied me out.

I was still rock hard and hadn't cum yet, and Wayne grabbed the lube and poured it all over my dick. I was still on my back, and he basically jumped on top of me and let my cock slide right into his hole. After him eating his cum out of my ass, I knew I wasn't going to last very long. He kept stroking his cock as he was riding mine, and I let out a loud gasp and shot my load right into his hole. He kept thrusting up and down, completely draining my vein deep into his ass. There was no way I was going to eat my load out of his ass, as tempting as it may be.

I was really surprised by how he acted and totally turned on. I had thought he was a total top, but I guess I was wrong.

"I never bottom, but there's just something about you that made me want it inside of me."

I had my very own lady in the streets, freak in the sheets guy, and I wasn't mad about it.

Chapter 5

After a few months of dating, my work schedule really started to slow down. I think my patients were noticing that I was no longer doing my typical sessions, and they quickly started transferring over to Chris and Danny, who were doing really well. It didn't bother me much, though, as it allowed me to spend way more time with Wayne.

We started talking about moving in together into his beach condo, and I was really excited about the thought of it. Things were on such a good track with us. Sure, we had our share of arguments and even went a few days without speaking once, but all in all, it was exactly what I had wanted.

We were planning a weekend away to an all-inclusive spa in the mountains, and I had one new patient who had specifically requested me. I had planned on passing him over to Chris but figured since it was a new patient that it would be best for me to do the intake. I waited for Rocky to bring him back to the therapy room and was shocked when I saw who it was.

Austin.

He shut the door as he walked in and approached me, trying to give me a hug. I pushed him away from me and told him he needed to get the fuck out of here.

"I'm so sorry Hunter. I don't know what I was thinking. I... I... I have no words. I have no excuse. I didn't do it to cause any harm. It's just something I've always done and it never crossed my mind to ask."

Sure, his video of us fucking didn't cause any harm. In fact, it lined my pockets with money. What I was more hurt about was how he just disappeared afterward.

"You fucking left me. You completely dropped off the face of the earth. I've moved on. I don't need this. You need to leave."

Austin sat down on the couch, and I could tell he had no intention of leaving. He looked so sad—almost pathetic. He just kept apologizing, and then it came out.

"I'm in love with you, Hunter. I don't know what to do without you."

"I really don't care, Austin. You hurt me in the worst way. You disappeared. I've moved on. I've met someone, and I have no intentions on looking at the past."

As hard as it was, I needed to let him go. Even with the history we had and the amazing sex, he was toxic, and I needed to get rid of him.

"I really need you to leave."

He got up off the couch and walked toward the door, and I sat back down. He grabbed the handle, but instead of opening it, he locked it.

"What are you doing, Austin?"

He turned around and started walking back toward me.

"What I should have done a long time ago."

I was still sitting on the couch as he quickly approached me. He leaned down and grabbed my face and started kissing me. I hesitated for a minute and tried pushing him away, but he wouldn't give up, and eventually I succumbed.

Kissing him was something I'd never forget. He shoved his tongue down my throat and I pulled him on top of me as we made out. He was straddled over my lap, holding on tightly to the back of my head as we continued to kiss. He pulled my shirt off and lowered his head, kissing my neck and making his way to my chest. I ripped his shirt off and started sucking on his nipples, pulling him as close to me as I could get him.

We must have made out for a solid twenty minutes in that same position. I picked him up and pushed him over so that he was lying down on the couch, pulling his pants and briefs off and diving down toward his cock. He was rock hard, and just as beautiful as I had remembered. I grabbed onto the base of his dick and swallowed the entire thing. He grabbed onto my hair, assisting my head as it went up and down and thrusting his hips into my face. With each thrust, I could feel his tool stretching out the back of my throat, and I was loving every moment of it.

I pushed down my pants and crawled up toward his face, holding onto the bottom of his chin while I guided my cock into his mouth. I held myself up with the arm of the couch and started fucking his face, shoving myself all the way into his mouth. He was grabbing onto my ass, slapping it, and pulling me into his face as fast as he could. He pushed me out of his mouth and I held my dick against my stomach so that he could suck on my balls, making his way down to my hole.

I propped myself up a bit so that I was sitting on his face, feeling him shoving his tongue deep into my hole. He spread my cheeks and dove in as deep as he could, and it felt like pure euphoria. I started jerking my cock and bent back down so I could shove it in his mouth. I wanted him to get it nice and wet before I took control.

I let him suck on my dick for a few more minutes, and then without saying anything, slid down in between his legs. I grabbed ahold of his legs and placed them over my shoulders, exposing his hole and bending his back so I could have easy access. I wasn't grabbing any lube. I spit in my hand and rubbed it on my hole, and then onto the tip of my cock. I shoved my member into his hole as fast as I could. He let out a loud scream, which was exactly what I wanted.

I waited a few seconds to let him adjust, and then started pounding away as fast as I could. He pulled me close to him so we could make out, but I could tell he was in a bit of pain because he wasn't doing much kissing. He was basically just resting his tongue in my mouth, trying to catch his breath. I pounded that hole for four or five minutes before pulling out and flipping him around so that he was flat on his stomach.

I dove down and sunk my tongue into his hole, shoving it in as deep as I could and licking my way down to his cock, and back up his balls to his hole again. He reached around and was holding onto the back of my head, and I ate that booty like my dinner. I slowly slid my way back up, kissing every inch of his back and rubbing my body against his as I made my way up to his neck. I started sucking on my neck and rubbing my dick against his ass, and I reached down so that I could guide it back into his hole.

I kept my body close to his as I started thrusting again, wrapping one arm around his neck and continuing to kiss him while I fucked his hole. His hole was so warm and inviting, I wanted to last as long as I could, but knew that wasn't going to happen. I kept on fucking him for another minute before I started flooding his hole, letting out one of the loudest screams I've ever let out. He started moving his hips, backing his ass into me, and milking me for every last drop.

I pulled my dick out and sat down on the couch, and he swung himself around and sucked the rest of the cum off of it. He stood up in front of me and started jerking off, grabbing onto the back of my head and pulling my mouth toward his tool. It wasn't even ten seconds before he was blowing his load in my face, and I opened my mouth to gladly accept his gift. I pulled him closer so I could suck the rest out of him, holding it in my mouth and pulling him down to kiss me. We started making out again, swapping his cum and letting it run down the sides of our mouths.

I didn't even say anything else to him after that. I knew he wasn't going to leave, so I put my clothes back on and just left.

And that was the last I ever heard from him. Again.

Chapter 6

It didn't really occur to me what had happened until I got home and realized I was supposed to meet Wayne for dinner. I felt horrible. I felt guilt. I felt disappointment. I had just fucked everything up and for nothing.

I knew I couldn't hide it from him, so I immediately called him and asked if he could meet at my house before dinner.

When he got there, I didn't even waste any time. I immediately told him what had happened and didn't stop apologizing. He just kind of sat there, not saying anything for a few minutes, and then finally looked at me.

"I did the same thing a few weeks ago."

I was shocked. What was he talking about? And then he started telling me more.

"My ex came over to pick up a few things he had left. I had been drinking, and one thing just led to another. Before I knew it, I was picking my clothes up from the floor and asking him to leave. I have no clue how it happened. I was waiting for the right time to tell you because I was so ashamed that I had fucked everything up. You're the greatest thing that has ever happened to me, and I fucked up."

He got up and started to walk toward the door. I grabbed his hand and led him back to the couch to sit back down. I gave him a hug and a kiss and asked where this left us.

He assumed I was going to break up with him, and I assumed he would break up with me. We sat for over an hour talking about it, realizing that we had both made mistakes and that we couldn't let this ruin what we had. I think we both knew that we had learned our lessons and would never let anything like this happen again.

I grabbed Wayne's hand and led him toward my bedroom. As I started taking off my shirt, Wayne knelt down on the floor and grabbed my hips and pulled me closer to him. He looked up at me and started rubbing on my cock through my pants. I pulled my shirt off and threw it on the bed and grabbed the back of his head and rubbed it while he started unzipping my pants. He pulled my pants down and pulled my cock through the opening of my briefs and started sucking on it. For a moment, I forgot how good he was at sucking dick.

He was going up and down my shaft pretty slowly, and I could feel the head of my cock going into his throat, which wasn't making him gag at all. He'd pull my cock out of his mouth and start sucking on my balls, stroking my cock and looking straight up at me. He was making a lot of noises while he was doing this, and I could tell that he had a little bit of a pig side to him.

I pushed him away from my cock and kind of forced him down on the ground, pulling out his dick so I could suck on it. I sucked on his cock for a while, and then lifted his legs above my head to arch his ass up a bit so I could start licking his hole. He had just a tiny bit of hair on his hole, which was a total turn on for me. I stuck my tongue in as deep as I could get it, and he started panting like a dog. The noises were a bit distracting, but also a turn on at the same time.

I licked his hole for a few minutes, occasionally sticking the tip on my finger inside, and then he reached over and opened my nightstand drawer. It's almost like he knew what I had in there. He grabbed a dildo out of the drawer and handed it to me. He said he wanted me to fuck him with the dildo while he sucked my dick. He was still lying on the ground, kind of arched up on the couch, and

I got on my knees and moved toward his face. Before I could stick the dildo in his ass, he grabbed the bottle of lube and literally poured it all over his chest. He then poured it all over mine and started rubbing it all over my chest and cock with his hands. For a second I thought he was going to want to wrestle, but I was super turned on by the way he was acting. It's almost like he wanted to make sure nothing else would interest me again.

I ran my hand across his chest to get some of the lube and rubbed it all over the dildo. I leaned over and slowly pushed it into his ass. He let out a loud moan, then grabbed my dick and started sucking on it. I moved the dildo in and out of his ass in a pretty normal pace, and he grabbed onto my hand and made me start thrusting it faster and faster. He kept on sucking my dick the entire time, and I was basically destroying his hole with the dildo. He grabbed the dildo from me and pulled it out of his ass and threw it across the room, looked at me and said, "Fuck me now." He was still panting and a bit out of breath.

He turned over and got on all fours so I would fuck him from behind. I was still a bit surprised. He had only bottomed for me once, but apparently he was really trying to make a point. He leaned over the seat of the couch, and I got up behind him and slid my dick right into his hole. I didn't even need to add any extra lube because he had it all over our bodies. Plus, my dick was dripping from him sucking on it. I grabbed onto his hips and thrust my cock in and out of his hole, just letting the head almost completely come out before shoving it back inside. I could tell he really liked this. I fucked him like this for a few minutes, and then he turned around and asked if I had a double ended dildo. Of course I did—every gay man does.

I had only ever used a double ended dildo with one other guy when I first moved to San Francisco. I grabbed it out of a different drawer and laid down on the ground with my head against the couch and let him take control. I spread my legs, and he got in front of me with his legs wrapped over mine and our dicks and balls basically touching. This double dildo was about 18 inches long, and not too thick, but thick enough to feel good. He poured more lube on us, and then wiped it all over the dildo. He slid it in my ass first, and my cock instantly shot up to attention. He then put the other end in his ass and almost instantly started moving his hips back and forth, which made the dildo start moving a little bit inside my ass.

The dildo felt incredible once I started moving my hips with his. I grabbed onto my cock and started stroking it while I was being dildo fucked. It felt like I was really taking it up the ass. He was still letting out loud moans, and between the dildo, our hips moving, and our legs rubbing against each other, I was completely turned on. We stayed like this for five or six minutes, and anytime I let go of my cock, he would grab onto it and stroke it. I'm not sure how I wasn't already cumming, but I must have mentally known he was going to want me to fuck him again.

Wayne stopped moving his hips and slowly pulled the dildo out of my ass. I didn't even say anything—I just stayed on my back waiting to see what his next move was. He pulled the dildo out of his own ass and came over and started sucking my dick again. He brought his head up and said, "Fuck me again."

I quickly got up and got behind him. He was on all fours again, so I just shoved my cock right in his ass and started pounding the fuck out of him. I could tell I was getting close to cumming, so I pulled out, grabbed the dildo, and started fucking him with his dildo. He kept on moaning and really liked it, probably because the dildo was just about the same size as my cock. I pushed it in and out for about a minute so I could re-gain some composure in my own dick. I was having way too much fun to cum and didn't want to stop.

I flipped him over on his back and put his legs above my shoulders. He grabbed my cock and guided it into his hole. At this point, his hole was pretty stretched out from my cock and the different dildos, so I knew I probably could fuck a while longer without risking shooting my load. He pulled me down and started kissing me while I was fucking him and kept making a lot of moaning and grunting noises.

After about another seven minutes of him grunting and me going to pound town on his ass, I knew I was getting close to cumming. He started stroking his cock and came about ten seconds later. About half of his cum shot up on my chest, which was really hot. I told him I was about to cum, and just as I was about to blow, I pulled my cock out of his ass. I didn't even have to grab my cock to jerk it to the finish—I immediately started shooting my load all over him. He grabbed my cock and started stroking it, and I must have shot eight or nine good loads before it finally died down.

He pulled me down and held me close to him with our bodies, lube and cum rubbing together. We laid there together all night, holding each other and kissing. And after this, I knew things were definitely going to work out between us.

Chapter 7

After making up, things were definitely back on the right path. I ended up moving in with him into his beach condo, and Jackie sold our house and bought her own on the other side of town. I had never really imagined that I would be the type to settle down, especially after all of the adventures that I found myself in. The practice was on autopilot; I hired two more full time therapists, and I only went in once a week to check on things and make sure they were following the compliance standards. The money was rolling in, and I was able to spend all of my time with Wayne.

Now, things were nowhere near perfect with Wayne. Sure, we were perfect for each other. However, our relationship was not.

Wayne had suffered some trauma as a child, although he never went into full details about what happened. As a therapist, I was pretty much able to diagnose him without him actually telling me, and even with my expertise, it sometimes became tough to manager.

We would get into screaming matches—mother fucking each other so loudly that the neighbors would be looking out their windows to make sure we were okay. Wayne would leave for days at a time, and then I would do the same thing. We were spending so much time together—too much time together—that we didn't always know how to deal with it. At the end of the day, we loved each other, and even with the disfunction, we were perfect together.

We moved out of Wayne's condo and bought our first home together in a cute community on a lake. The house was perfect, and it was our first major purchase together. We were a bit farther outside of the city, which probably wasn't the greatest idea, because we were still spending too much time together.

It seemed that the more time we spent together, the more insecure Wayne became in our relationship. The whole cheating situation that we had found ourselves in was constantly being brought up, even though we had both promised to never speak about it again. He would bring it up, we'd make up, and then a few days later, I would bring it up, and then make up again. It was a roller coaster, but I sure did love a good ride.

We had one fight that was particularly bad—probably the worst we had ever had. Wayne was in a really bad mood, and just had a tone in his voice that was so condescending. At that point, I wasn't even sure what we were arguing about, but I was sure it was something stupid. He said something to me and the tone in his voice just completely rubbed me the wrong way, and I snapped. And by snapped, I mean "flipped the fuck out."

I started slamming doors and throwing things, telling him how much I fucking hated him and wished that we had never met. I packed a bag, but he wouldn't let me leave. I threw the bag in the bathroom and grabbed my keys and ran out the door, but he stood behind my car like a crazy person. I was damn near tempted to just run him over, but we didn't need that on top of everything else. I ran back inside the house and called his mother, which just made matters worse.

The fight went on for hours until one of us finally fell asleep (I don't even remember which of us fell asleep first). And then the next morning was like any other morning—like nothing had ever happened. Wayne woke up and was all sweet, and for a moment, I forgot anything had even happened. He said he had planned a picnic for us at a park and told me to get ready. He didn't normally plan events like this, so I was a bit surprised but figured that

I'd go with it. I hopped in the shower while he packed a backpack, and then we were off.

We arrived at this park on a lake, and it was completely desolate. I was surprised that it was so dead for a Sunday but didn't care because I really wasn't in the mood to be around other people. There was a boardwalk that went through the woods, so we decided to walk it to see where it led to.

The boardwalk went on forever and never seemed to end. After about ten minutes, Wayne grabbed my hand and turned me around toward him, pulled me into his arms, and started making out with me. This was his way of making up, and I knew what was going to come next.

He pushed me up against the boardwalk rail and kept kissing me, sticking his hands down my pants and grabbing onto my dick. I grabbed onto the top of his shoulders and pushed him down to his knees so he could start blowing me.

He pulled my shorts down and grabbed onto my cock and started stroking it, licking the tip of my head before taking the entire thing in his mouth. I grabbed onto the rails behind me to hold myself up. There was something about the wilderness and the excitement of getting caught that really had me going, and I knew that I wanted him to plow my ass.

I let him slobber on my knob for a few minutes and then turned around so that he could get my hole ready. I leaned over the boardwalk railing, and he dove his face straight into my ass. His beard tickled a bit because he hadn't shaved in a few weeks, but his tongue caressing my hole felt like heaven. I felt him stick a few fingers in to get it loosened up, and then he stood up, pulled his pants down and shoved his dick deep inside.

He had me so wet from eating it that we didn't even need lube. I was hanging onto the railing with my chest bent over it while he held on tight to my hips, thrusting his cock deep into my hole. He reached his hand around and covered my mouth because I was screaming pretty loud, and then stopped fucking me for a minute because we both heard something.

We both stood there as still as we could, in silence, until the distant conversation disappeared. We thought for sure that we were about to be caught, and as soon as I couldn't hear the noise anymore, I started rocking my hips back and forth to get the momentum going again. I started jerking my dick while he was plowing me from behind, and within moments was shooting my load off the boardwalk and into the water below. Wayne kept pumping at my hole and when he said he was about to cum, I pushed him out and turned around, getting down on my knees and letting him blow his load all over my face. He grabbed onto the back of my head and shoved his cock in my mouth so I could get the last drop, and then picked me up to start making out again.

He grabbed a towel out of his backpack so that I could wipe off my face and handed me my shorts to put back on. I started walking back in the direction that we had come from, talking about how hot that was, but Wayne wasn't responding. I turned around and immediately started crying when I saw what Wayne was doing.

He was down on one knee, ring in hand, holding a chalkboard.

"Will you marry me?"

Chapter 8

I walked back toward Wayne, and when I was close enough, he grabbed my hand and slipped the ring on my finger. It was a beautiful ring—white gold with five diamonds. I couldn't speak, but just started nodding "yes" and picked him up so that I could kiss him again. I couldn't believe that this was happening. Even with all of our arguments and all of our issues, Wayne was the man I was meant to spend the rest of my life with.

As soon as we got home from the park, I called my family and some of my closest friends. I was so over the moon that I couldn't wait to tell anyone, and I actually wanted to start planning the wedding immediately. I didn't want to wait. This was the man I had waited for my entire life, and I wasn't going to waste any time.

We started doing some research and found the perfect wedding planner who specialized in mountain weddings. We were both huge fans of the mountains and even started talking about moving there. The following weekend, we took a trip to the mountains to meet the wedding planner, and I swear we fell in love all over again.

They venue she showed us was breathtaking. It was a mountain resort with the wedding venue at the summit of the mountain. The ceremony would take place outdoors on the edge of the mountain, and we could see for miles and miles. The reception would take place in the lodge. It was made of wood logs with huge floor-to-ceiling windows overlooking the mountain range and steep vaulted ceilings. I closed my eyes and could literally picture our wedding day and just how perfect it would be.

We decided to do things a little differently and opted out of having a wedding party. At the end of the day, no one really likes the hassle that comes with being in a wedding, and everyone was so special to us that we didn't want to have to pick. Of course, though, I asked Rocky to say a speech because he really was my best friend, and we had been through so much together since moving to San Francisco.

We set a wedding date, and a few months later decided that it was time to leave California to go back to a slower-paced life. The decision came so quickly that I didn't even have time to say goodbye to my friends. Before I knew it, we had sold the first home that we had purchased together and were embarking on a journey across the country back to Pennsylvania. I really wanted to be closer to my family, and Wayne knew how important that was to me.

We bought a pretty big house on a nice chunk of land far enough outside of the city but close enough for easy access. This move was exactly what our relationship needed. Ever since getting engaged, things had gotten much better, although we still had occasional blow-ups.

We didn't have much time to settle in, and the wedding had been fast approaching. We had to make a few trips back to the mountains to meet with the wedding planner and iron out some final details, and each trip made me more and more excited for our upcoming nuptials. Our wedding was the highlight of the season, not only to our friends and families, but to the location as well, as they considered me to be a celebrity. I actually had to pull the owner of the resort aside the first time we met, because I needed to make it clear that anything he had heard about me would not play true to my interaction with him. His entire staff was extremely flirtatious, and I knew that they knew who I was, and it wasn't going to happen.

Our wedding day arrived, and it was quite honestly the most magical day of my life. The wedding planner went above and beyond to exceed my expectations, and I swear it was like a movie in itself. There had to have been over a thousand candles between the ceremony and reception, and they surprised us with fireworks during our first dance. I don't think there was a single person there with a dry eye—all the gays were crying because they realized I was no longer single, and then the straights were crying because that's just what they do at weddings.

It was such a beautiful day, and we left the following week for our honeymoon—two weeks on a private island in the Maldives.

And so we come to the end of my story— my fairytale. You now know more about my life than anyone does. Quite frankly, I've shared more with you than I've shared with anyone else, and I hope you've enjoyed the journey. This is Dr. Cage. I'm still a Sex Therapist—but now I'm off to the next chapter of my life.

I hope to see you soon.

Author Bio

Grayson Ace has had his fair share of sexcapades, and figured why not write about them? Recently divorced, he is re-discovering himself (and plenty of hot men) and creating many new sexy adventures along the way. If you like what you see, please leave a review, and you never know….you may end up in one of the stories!

GraysonAce.com
Facebook: Grayson Ace
Instagram: graysonaceofficial
Twitter: @GraysonAce1

More Books From

Grayson Ace

How I Got Here
First Year Out of the Closet
You're Only a Top?
You're Only a Bottom?
I Think I'm a Serial Swiper
Lookin' in All the Wrong Places
What Makes Me a Whore?
Back Door Pass
My European Adventure
A Breach in Confidentiality
An Unexpected Affair
Finding True Love
More to come!

More books from 4 Horsemen Publications

Erotica

Ali Whippe

Office Hours
Tutoring Center
Athletics
Extra Credit
Financial Aid
Bound for Release
Fetish Circuit
Now You See Me
Sexual Playground
Swingers
Discovered

Aria Skylar

Twisted Eros

Chastity Veldt

Molly in Milwaukee
Irene in Indianapolis
Lydia in Louisville
Natasha in Nashville
Alyssa in Atlanta
Betty in Birmingham
Carrie on Campus
Jackie in Jacksonville

Dalia Lance

My Home on Whore Island
Slumming It on Slut Street
Training of the Tramp
The Imperfect Perfection
Spring Break
72% Match
It Was Meant To Be... Or Whatever

Honey Cummings

Sleeping with Sasquatch
Cuddling with Chupacabra
Naked with New Jersey Devil
Laying with the Lady in Blue
Wanton Woman in White

Beating it with Bloody Mary
Beau and Professor Bestialora
The Goat's Gruff
Goldie and Her Three Beards
Pied Piper's Pipe
Princess Pea's Bed
Pinocchio and the Blow Up Doll
Jack's Beanstalk
Pulling Rapunzel's Hair
Curses & Crushes

NICK SAVAGE

The Fairlane Incidents
The Fortunate Finn Fairlane
The Fragile Finn Fairlane

NOVA EMBERS

A Game of Sales
How Marketing Beats Dick
Certified Public Alpha (CPA)
On the Job Experience
My GIF is Bigger than Your GIF
Power Play
Plugging in My USB
Hunting the White Elephant
Caution: Slippery When Wet

LGBT Erotica

Dominic N. Ashen
Steel & Thunder
Storms & Sacrifice
Secrets & Spires
Arenas & Monsters
My Three Orc Dads: a Novella

Eskay Kabba
Hidden Love
Not So Hidden

Grayson Ace
How I Got Here
First Year Out of the Closet
You're Only a Top?
You're Only a Bottom?
I Think I'm a Serial Swiper
Lookin in All the Wrong Places
What Makes Me a Whore?
A Breach in Confidentiality
Back Door Pass

My European Adventure
An Unexpected Affair
Finding True Love

LEO SPARX
Before Alexander
Claiming Alexander
Taming Alexander
Saving Alexander
The Case of Armando

ROBERT LEWIS
Someone to Love
Someone to Come Home To

DISCOVER MORE AT
4HorsemenPublications.com

www.ingramcontent.com/pod-product-compliance
Lightning Source LLC
Chambersburg PA
CBHW031416310726
48971CB00003B/888